THE MONSTER WHO ATE THE STATE

WRITTEN AND ILLUSTRATED BY

CHRIS BROWNE

SOUTH DAKOTA HISTORICAL SOCIETY PRESS / PIERRE

Illustration page 26 © 2014 South Dakota Historical Society Press.

All other illustrations and text © 2014 Chris Browne.

This publication is funded, in part, by the Great Plains Education Foundation, Inc., Aberdeen, S.Dak.

Library of Congress Control Number: 2014946605

August 2014

Printed by We SP Corp., Seoul, Korea

41720-0 WESP-140502

Text and cover design by Angela Corbo Gier

Please visit our website at www.sdshspress.com.

Printed in Canada

21 20 19 18 17 2 3 4 5 6

This book is dedicated to the children of South Dakota, past, present, and future.

Roa

2

Something loud was coming up from an old mine shaft at the underground research lab in the Black Hills of South Dakota.

It was Soozy the dinosaur. She had just woken up from a long, long nap. And she was HUNGRY!

The world sure had changed! Where were the other dinosaurs? Where were the swamps and giant ferns? Soozy sniffed the air—and followed her nose to . . .

3

. . . Deadwood!

The streets were full of gunslingers
whose spurs jingled when they walked.
Good smells drifted out of some of the
buildings. Soozy stuck her nose in to
grab some lunch. The man at the door
told her to leave. They did not have a
table big enough for her!

4

Soozy heard roaring in the distance. Was it her friends? She ran
toward the sound. No! It was thousands and thousands of motorcycles
at the rally in Sturgis! She tried to eat a motorcycle. It tasted awful!

Soozy had to find something to eat. Her stomach was grumbling
louder than the motorcycles!

She saw four giants peering through the trees. Perhaps they could tell her where to eat.

Tourists screamed as Soozy came into view, but the faces seemed kind. They looked off to the south. Was there food in that direction? Soozy's stomach rumbled again as she started off.

She trotted down the highway until she saw a big man on
an ENORMOUS horse. The man pointed off into the distance.
Soozy took his advice and went that way.

She spied a herd of American bison in a field of prairie grass. She ran towards them, but they ran away. Ring-necked pheasants flew up out of the grass.

Soozy tried to follow them but the land began to change.

Gray hills with pink streaks rose like fortresses around her. She was in the Badlands. It was strange and beautiful, but the only sound she heard was her stomach. *Grumble*. She hurried on.

Then she saw someone she knew!

A green apatosaurus stood high on the next hill. Soozy ran over to him.

"Hello, Long Neck! How are you? Where is everybody?"

She gave him a big hug, but Long Neck said nothing. His skin was cold and hard against her cheek. She looked into his green face.

He was not real! He was just a statue.

APATOSAURUS

Soozy sighed.

She was alone again. She walked on with her head down for a long time.

13

In a town called Mitchell, she finally found something to eat! It was a palace made out of corn! She crammed a panel into her mouth. It was tasty!

But it could use a little salt and butter, she thought. It was so dry that now she was thirsty too.

At the edge of a big town called Sioux Falls, she spied
another dinosaur! He stood at the bottom of a deep rock quarry.
"Yoo hoo! Tallboy!" Soozy roared and waved her claw.
Soozy asked him politely if he knew where she could get
a drink of water. Tallboy just stared off into space.

"*Phony!*" Soozy huffed and walked away.

Her throat was so dry that her roars were coming out in whispers. Soozy heard the babble of a waterfall. Something to drink at last!

Visitors to Falls Park were astonished to see Soozy lumbering toward the falls. She crouched beside the rushing water and took a long drink.

Aaahh!

she thought, that's what I needed.

"Roar, Roar,"

she tested her voice as she moved
through town. It was working just
fine again. The sound of bell chimes
answered her when she walked past
the Old Courthouse clock tower.
The spires of Saint Joseph's Cathedral
soared above the town.

Whoop! Whoop! Whoop!

A news helicopter swooped near Soozy's head. She almost tripped over one of the sculptures on the street as she looked up.

19

Soozy saw bright flashes ahead. The sign for the
State Theatre looked just like a piece of apple pie.
She bit into it. It was crunchy but not very filling!
Someone screamed . . .

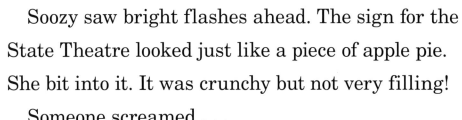

"The monster is
eating the State!"

20

21

Soozy sniffed the air. What was that smell? Was it cookies? If there was one thing Soozy loved more than long naps, it was cookies. Her nose led her to a hospital that looked like a castle.

Children stood on the towers and tossed cookies down to Soozy!

Then she waved her tail goodbye. The children waved back.

Time for a short nap. Soozy found a perfect meadow to curl up in at the Great Plains Zoo.

The zookeeper called a paleontologist from the college to look at her. The professor examined Soozy.

"She is a Fallsosaurus," he declared, "because she has made her home in Sioux Falls."

Soozy liked her new home. The rhinos reminded her of her old pal triceratops. The giraffes were as tall as an apatosaurus. Well, almost. Best of all—they were real.

The people welcomed her to their town. She promised she would always play nice as long as she had milk and cookies and children to visit her. And she did.

The End

1 (Page 2) **The Sanford Underground Laboratory** is 4,850 feet under the ground at Lead, South Dakota. The lab is in an old gold mine, where scientists now look for dark matter.

2 **Dinosaurs lived over sixty million years ago.** A famous Tyrannosaurus rex was found near Faith, South Dakota, in 1990. Its nickname is Sue, and it is now in the Field Museum in Chicago.

3 (Page 4) **Deadwood** is the site of the Black Hills gold rush that started in 1874. The most famous gunslinger was Wild Bill Hickok.

4 (Page 5) **The Sturgis Motorcycle Rally** takes place every August. It is the largest annual rally in the world.

5 (Pages 6–7) **Mount Rushmore** is near Keystone, South Dakota. Gutzon Borglum carved the heads of four presidents into the mountain. Each head is sixty feet tall.

6 (Page 8) **Crazy Horse** was a famous Lakota Indian leader. Korczak Ziolkowski began carving the mountain, and his family continues to work on it. The sculpture will be 641 feet long and 563 feet high when it is finished.

7 (Page 9) **Custer State Park** in the Black Hills of South Dakota is the second largest state park in the United States. It is home to buffalo, prairie dogs, and many other animals.

(Page 9) **American bison, or buffalo,** roamed the Plains in huge herds until humans hunted them almost to extinction. Today bison are making a comeback. There are fifteen hundred of them in Custer State Park.

(Page 9) **The ring-necked pheasant** is the state bird of South Dakota. Pheasants originally came from Asia.

8 (Page 10) The rock formations in **Badlands National Park** are the result of ancient deposits and erosion. Different deposits of soil have different colors—gray, pink, tan, or black.

9 (Pages 11–13) The statue of the apatosaurus is eighty feet long. It greets visitors at the entrance to **Wall, South Dakota**.

10 (Page 14) **The Corn Palace of Mitchell** celebrates the farmers of the state and the crops they grow. The palace was first built in 1892.

11 (Page 15) **Sioux Falls** Many of the historic buildings in South Dakota are made from a pink stone called **quartzite**. Quarries near Sioux Falls are a major source of this stone.

(Pages 16–17) **The Big Sioux River** falls over many levels of quartzite boulders to form a waterfall.

(Page 18) The clock tower on the old **Minnehaha County Courthouse** and **Saint Joseph's Cathedral** are two of the historic buildings of Sioux Falls.

(Page 19) Sculptors from all over the world bring their work to Sioux Falls for **the Sculpture Walk**. The artwork is different each year.

(Pages 20–21) **The State Theatre** first opened in 1926. The people of Sioux Falls have spent time and money to reopen it.

(Pages 22–23) Not all important buildings are old. Today, sick and injured children receive care at **Sanford Children's Castle of Care Hospital** in Sioux Falls.

(Pages 24–26) Over one thousand animals from around the world live in the **Great Plains Zoo**. There are giraffes, tigers, monkeys, and a rare black rhino.

Further Reading

Anderson, William. *M is for Mount Rushmore: A South Dakota Alphabet.* Illus. Cheryl Harness. Chelsea, Mich.: Sleeping Bear Press, 2005.

Feeny, Kathy. *South Dakota Facts and Symbols.* Mankato, Minn.: Hilltop Books, 2001.

Hughes, Catherine D. *National Geographic Little Kids First Big Book of Dinosaurs.* Washington, D.C.: National Geographic Children's Books, 2011.

Latza, Jodi Holley. *South Dakota: An Alphabetical Scrapbook.* Photo. Greg Latza. Sioux Falls, S.Dak.: PeopleScapes Publishing, 2000.

Meierhenry, Mark, and David Volk. *The Mystery of the Maize.* Illus. Marty Two Bulls, Sr. Pierre: South Dakota State Historical Society Press, 2010.

Meierhenry, Mark, and David Volk. *The Mystery of the Pheasants.* Illus. Susan Turnbull. Pierre: South Dakota State Historical Society Press, 2012.

Patrick, Jean L. S. *Who Carved the Mountain?: The Story of Mount Rushmore.* Illus. Renée Graef. Keystone, S.Dak.: Mount Rushmore History Assoc., 2005.

Relf, Pat. *A Dinosaur Named SUE™: The Story of the Colossal Fossil.* New York: Scholastic Inc., 2000.